Whole Heap o' Troubles

By

Kevin James Donoghue

The Great Book of Alchemy

The Adventures of Robyn Nudd
Part I

A 5th Worlde Saga

1st edition

In Mermory of Richard Greene

Who introduced me to tales of adventure.

A note from the author

The Great Book of Alchemy and the Adventures of Robyn Nudd are a collection of sagas from the 5th Worlde. These sagas are not a series of historical novels, and whilst many of the characters have indeed appeared in the history of your world, in the 5th Worlde, their histories are completely different and a substantial amount of imagination has been used to ensure this fact.

The Bells of the Watch

Number of Bells	Bell Pattern	Middle Watch	Morning Watch	Forenoon Watch	After-noon Watch	Dog Watch First	Dog Watch Last	First Watch
one	1	0.30	4.30	8.30	12.30	16.30		20.30
two	2	1.00	5.00	9.00	13.00	17.00		21.00
three	2 1	1.30	5.30	9.30	13.30	17.30		21.30
four	2 2	2.00	6.00	10.00	14.00	18.00		22.00
five	2 2 1	2.30	6.30	10.30	14.30		18.30	22.30
six	2 2 2	3.00	7.00	11.00	15.00		19.00	23.00
seven	2 2 2 1	3.30	7.30	11.30	15.30		19.30	23.30
eight	2 2 2 2	4.00	8.00	12.00	16.00		20.00	24.00

The Adventures of Robyn Nudd
Part 1

A Whole Heap o' Troubles

1

Sunday Morning, Camden Town

Robyn Nudd; and the Sheriff of Nottingham are moored at Camden Lock, London, NW1 8AF.

The Sunday morning sun spread its early morning gaze over the city of London. And indeed across Camden Town. Yet most importantly of all its golden rays fell gracefully upon the Sheriff of Nottingham, whose big, fat and substantially round bottom snuggled cosily, drown in slumber, not wishing to relinquish the night.

You know how it is when you are still half a sleep? That dream like state between wakefulness and the moment you are actually conscious of the fact that you have awoken? Well I was somewhere near there. I stretched languidly and yawned. I moved a lazy arm slowly up to the top of my head and scratched at my messy brown thatch gently. My tongue felt

like newly sanded parchment. And there was a taste
in my mouth…and it really was no taste at all. Well
no…that's not actually true. It tasted like what I
imagined the bottom of the cage in which a friend of
mine lets a strange old magpie, called Oda, stay.

Yes…that's what it tasted like. I think. I mean the
magpie's accommodation and not my friend obviously. Look…what I mean to say, in my befuddled
early morning-headed way, is that; an odd magpie
called Oda sometimes likes to stay with my friend
Lady Yvette. Lady Yvette has had specially con-
structed and wonderfully luxurious accommodation
for such occasions.

I guardedly opened one eye and blinked softly as
the suns rays floated about the cabin. After a moment or so I managed to focus. I peered around
the small cabin in which I slept. Eventually my eye
found the starboard porthole. It was situated just
above the waterline and rocked gently up and down.

Another eye looked back at me. It was black. All
black. And it was surrounded by bloated white flesh.
Shocked, I heaved my head backwards with such a
jerk that it made my brain hurt. Slowly I opened my
other or, if you will, second eye.

The eye that looked back at me began to slide
across the porthole. As it did it revealed a squashed
and broken nose. Part of a mouth appeared directly
below it. This was accompanied by a dull echoing
thud on the side of the boat.

It was a truly bizarre moment. I held a scream silently in my mind. I twisted my body and slipped out
of the warm comfortable bed. Still naked, I moved
quickly across to the porthole for a better look. The
view, now a close up, had not improved. The eye was
still there. It looked like a cold fried egg swimming in
a plate of congealed bacon fat with the smallest piece
of tomato smeared around the edges. Huevos Ran-

chero; as it's called in España.

It was an eye that had, quite frankly, seen better days. Not recently obviously...but somewhere in the not too distant past. Now...I know that you know that I'm a vegetarian. And so this was definitely not a good start to the morning. I really do prefer a warm bread roll and some hot coffee. Moving across the cabin I pulled on a pair of woollen hose and rough spun chemise. Then I carefully checked my eyeliner in the looking glass before I opened the hatch and crept out onto the stern deck. I took a long look around the dockside and breathing in deeply I took a healthy sniff of the fresh Camden Town morning air. There was no one about. In fact, I realised, it was still very early; only about the sixth bell of the morning watch. Even the anglers had not begun to arrive yet. That was a good sign. Not that they ever came this close to the lock. It was not a very good place for fishing.

Today; all was quiet and still. There were only three other boats moored along the bank. I listened to the gentle lapping of the water as a soft breeze blew along the Regent's Canal. I remember thinking that no one from the street could possibly see this far along the lock. And so I pulled myself up on to the roof of the boat and moved quickly along the top plank, towards the bow. I collected a pole, which was kept near the outer rail, as I went and dropped it down towards the cabin's porthole. It struck something firm. I leaned my head over the side and looking down into the murky water. I could just see the body. It was floating next to the barge and bobbing gently in the water ~ like a cork in a baby's bath.

'Shit...' I murmured to myself.

'...This is serious. What do you do when a body appears next to your boat first thing on a Sunday morning? There ought to be a law against it!'

I did some hard thinking. I was sure it wasn't there last night…but well, you know how it is? To be honest…I couldn't be really sure. The beer in The Hawley is rather too good…and in honesty…I couldn't swear to the fact.

'Shit, and double shit!'

It was with the gentlest of pushes that I thrust the pole against the body and watched as it floated away from the boat.

'The Dibble is going to be all over this. And there is no way that I can run…unless…'

'Morning Robyn, what's that you got?'

It was old Sam. He was a grey bearded codger who had his boat, The Dancing Queen, permanently tied to the moorings at Camden Lock. His scrawny neck stretched up from the hatch of the Dancing Queen and peered at me. All the while he searched his waistcoat for his eye lenses.

'Looks like a body to me. Let me try and get me eyes holes focused.'

'Double shit…with knobs on!' I said under my breath.

'It is a body Sam. Best call for the dibble.'

'Not me!' Said Sam. And he disappeared ~ like a rabbit down a hole. The hatch of the Dancing Queen slammed shut with a loud bang and I heard the scrape of the bolt as it slid across.

'Shit.' I said again. It was becoming the word of the morning.

'Mornin'.' The angler said as he walked along the towpath.

'Excuse me mate. Give the dibble a holler will ya? Sharpish like. I just found a mush in the cut.'

The angler turn as pale as a ghost and shaking his head said;

'Oh no…that will not be good for the fishing. They will have had a right nosh up already. I'm off back to me gaff. Don't get me involved.' And he made a quick about turn.

'Shit, shit, and double shit!'

2

The Men They Couldn't Hang

Robyn Nudd; and the Sheriff of Nottingham are moored at Camden Lock, Camden Town, London, NW1 8AF

I knew it would not take long for the dibble to arrive. So it was time to move. And I had to move quickly. North of the Gap; a certain element of society use 'The Lingo'. It means we can communicate secretly with each other and that there is less fear of informants and spies. This helps us avoid the attention of the 'Men of the Watch', who we always called the 'Plod' and their officers ~ the 'Dibble'.

The 'Quizzers' are something else again. Half empire and half church; they are members of the Inquisition. Still there is little difference between them all. They are all kings men; mean, savage, violent bullies. And we hate them more than we do the Templars.

'The dibble will be all over me in about two minutes,' I thought;

'Best move this body…and see to my stash.'

Slowly I pushed the body away from the Sheriff. I pushed it as far as the pole would reach. It drifted out into the middle of the canal. It took a lot of effort. I was breathing heavily when, to my amazement, the body started to float right back toward me. I stared in disbelief and shook my head.

I replaced the pole on the roof's starboard rail and nipped down to the bow. Taking my key, which I kept on a lanyard around my neck, I swiftly opened the bow hatch. I then entered the boat from the front or as we bargees call it, the bow hatch. I quickly checked that all the holds were safe, secure, and secretly hidden.

'The last thing you need is the dibble nosing around when you have a boat full of contraband.' I said softly to myself.

Soon I was happy that everything was as secure as it could possible be. I took stock of my situation. There was no easy way out of this predicament. So as Judy used to say;

'look good, feel good, do good.'

Thinking of Judy gave me pause for a moment. Judy Teen was a huge influence in my life. She had bought me from my father, when I was nearly three, and she had brought me up in her brothel, a cozy inn, on the quayside of the Liverpool docks. It had been a good life; looking after the ladies. Warm, clean work, with plenty of food and somewhere safe to sleep. And it was a true introduction to the street life…which was the lot of the poorer city folk.

And so I followed Judy's instructions; it was time to change out of my work clothes; a loose, rough spun chemise and shortened hoes, and into my best clothes; a loose, rough spun chemise and shortened hoes. I threw some smack on ~ like an artist throws paint around a canvas. Then carefully applied my lippy…before heading up to the deck and sprightly jumping ashore.

The early morning sun danced lightly on the waters of the canal. The barges rocked gently to and fro on their moorings and the painted lock tops gleamed, a brilliant bright white. Even the cobbles of the lock path seemed to glisten as I headed towards the steps and taking them two at a time I climbing up from the towpath and out of the canal gate.

And suddenly I was there; Camden High Street. The Devil's Cauldron, the world famous music venue, stood to my left. It was immersed in a shabby shadow of early morning gloom. A short, squat, yet still impressive building. It had recently had painted across its doors the words;

'Closed by Order of the Ministry.'

I shook my head in despair. Another example of these damned 'Cultural Laws.' Oh, how the dibble loved these new laws. They enforcing them with an unprecedented zeal. Smiling with a gloating satisfaction ~ the way that bullies always do. It was no exaggeration to say that they enjoyed their work.

These 'Cultural Laws' had come into force in the last few months and the people where very unhappy with them. There was trouble brewing. You didn't have to be a seer to know that.

Me…I'm the quite type. You know, sullen, reflective, and moody. I liked to keep a low profile; so I do as Judy has taught me.

'Keep your nose clean, your head down, and get on with your work.' She always said to me. This was usually followed by a slap around the chops or a swift kick to the pants. And so I learned the rules to live my life by…and I put them into good practise. As any young smuggler would. For I was one of 'The men they couldn't hang.' Of the female variety obviously; Yet still one of the 'Gentlemen.'

Cultural Laws…I shit 'em. I mean…what was the point of a law if you couldn't find the wriggle room. That's how the world works, right? The king makes a rule…the dibble enforce it. And we gentlemen… well, we find a small gap in the fence, as it were…a slight crack in the window glass ~ the space between the light and the dark. The shadow. Working in the shadows allows us to carry on exactly as we had before; ignoring the laws entirely. Just as the old song says. I started to sing;

> *'If you wake at midnight, and hear a
> horse's feet,*
> *Don't go drawing back the blind, or
> looking in the street,*
> *Them that ask no questions isn't told
> a lie.*
> *Watch the wall my darling while the
> Gentlemen go by. '*
>
> *'Five and twenty ponies,*
> *Trotting through the dark ~*
> *Brandy for the Parson, 'Baccy for the
> Clerk.*
> *Laces for a lady; letters for a spy,*
> *Watch the wall my darling while the
> Gentlemen go by!'*

Now just a few strides away from the lock gate is the bridge. The bridge stretches gracefully over the canal. On the other side of the bridge I could see the alarm point. These alarm points are also new. They are tall, box shaped, cubicles. A bit like an extra large coffin that has been stood upright…on its end. They are painted a bright red. And just to ensure that you realised that this box is an alarm point…they have the words 'Alarm Point' painted in black on their front and sides.

During daylight, the 'Plod' stand guard here. So as to be able to monitor the traffic as it crossed the bridge and before it can approach London proper. But at this hour…the gates to the city being closed… the streets are deserted. On the inside of these alarm points, near the roof, is a metal triangle. It has a beater attached to it by a short length of chain.

I felt my stomach churning as I approached it. It seemed to me that I was about to do something that I knew I was going to regret. And yet…I really had no choice. I could think of absolutely no alternative. At least two people had seen me with the body. And if I knew that two people had seen me…well then…that meant that at least ten others would have seen me too!

'In London town; the walls have ears…and sometimes they have eyes…' I said softly as I approached the alarm point. I took the beater in my hand, released a deep sigh before breathing deeply and then I made the beater swing from side to side.

3

The Dibble

Robyn Nudd; is at the Alarm Point, Camden bridge, Camden Town, London, NW1 8AF

The delightful chirping of the late rising Sunday song birds floated easily on the light morning breeze. It was drowned out by the terrible metal clanging. The noise reverberated along the length and breath of Camden High Street. I stuck a finger in my ear, like a tavern singer, and waggled it about a bit, as I waited for the noise to begin to fade. It was immediately replaced by the harsh sounds of shrill whistles. Before you could declare; 'Well I'll go to the top of our stairs…' the plod had surrounded me. The first two raised their spears and pushed me back against the wall of the bridge. The third held a small crossbow. It was slung low from his hip.

'Name!' he demanded.

'Robyn Mary Nudd. Female. Classified; Unfit for Military Service. Located: North of the Gap. Sheffield, Industrial Zone. No fixed abode. Bargee.'

I stated simply; keeping to the usual routine and knowing that deviating, in any fashion, would only cause me pain.

'Make your report.'

'There is a body in the canal.' I stated simply.

'An officer will be here soon. Don't you dare move!'

'Great, three plod and a dibble.' I remained silent

and smiled my secret smile.

The constables were behind me as I turned. They blocked the path with their heavy bodies. Their large spears held ready to strike. Their very existence radiating a vibrant intimidation. They waited, eagerly hoping, wishing, that I would make a break for it. Their eyes locked on me. I felt the malice sweeping across my body. Their eyes filing with lust and desire…and the desire was tinged with an edgy, anxious violence. I started to sweat.

'Place your hands on your head…and kneel.' The largest of the plod said; still holding his crossbow and positioning it close…aimed at my belly.

'A slow wound,' I thought;

'This one has been trained. Hurt them…but don't kill them too quickly, we need to gather information from them first.'

I sank to my knees and placed my hands on my head. I watched the second plod, the shorter of the three, as he moved to my rear and quickly frisked me.

'Clean.' He stated disappointedly.

'OK, I will take over.' Said the officer as he arrived on the bridge.

'You wish to make a report?' He stated.

'Tell me simply. What do you wish to report?'

'I found a body in the canal.' A short reply.

'Show me.' He responded.

I stood slowly keeping my hands away from my body and looking him straight in the eye. I led the way back across the bridge and along the towpath. Officer Dibble walked next to me. The plodding constables falling in behind. Their crossbows and spears held ready for action. We approached the moored barges.

'Explain the situation.' Ordered the officer.

'The Sheriff of Nottingham was softly sleeping. I

was curled up, cosy like…snuggling. Her big round bottom keeping me warm.' I explained with a quirky smile.

'When I woke I could see the body through the porthole. It was floating next to the barge.'

'You spent the night in sin and you admit it?' The shocked officer asked.

'There was no sin. I just slept.' I said simply.

'Where is this deviant? This Sheriff?' The officer demanded.

'You are standing right next to her.' And I quickly leapt aboard the barge.

'Isn't she beautiful?'

I took a long deep bow. The officer looked along the length of the barge and walk slowly up the gangplank. Then he stepped aboard The Sheriff of Nottingham.

'It is dangerous to toy so with the Ministry. You are already a 'Person of Interest' to us. I will add to your file this tendency of yours towards the unnatural, the immoral, and illegal relationships. And that you find it amusing to play your games with our authority. You may live to regret that jest!' He said to me.

He razed his hand and struck me on the head to emphasise his displeasure. It was a hard blow. It knocked me to the floor. The ring on his hand bit deeply into my skin. He saw the pain as it seeped into my eyes and a deep smile spread across his thin face.

'And so have many a witch regretted their action… as the fires licked their skin, and they bu-rn-ed!' He slurred the last word lovingly ~ stretching it out like a baker kneading his morning dough.

'Search!' He gave the constables a simple, sharp order.

One of them rushed on board and down into the Sheriff. He took a kick at me, accidentally on purpose, as he passed. Once inside he started to open draws and cabinets and as he went he overturned as much of the furniture as was possible.

'Show me the body.' Said the officer more softly.

I tugged my forelock and kept my head low, spitting the blood from my mouth, and wiping it with the back of my bare arm.

'That should take their mind off my stash.'

'Here.' I pointed to the water as I rubbed the side of my head.

The body was still bobbing up and down in the water. It was only a small length away from the Sheriff. It had slowly drifted nearer to the gap between the two barges and again I smiled.

'Now that looks less suspicious.'

The officer shouted an order to the remaining constables and they took the poles as instructed.

'Bring the body to the side and get it out of there. I need to look at it properly. You. Inside.'

Once inside the cabin, I stood and watched the plod as he turned out my belongings.

'Explain why you are here.' Said the dibble.

'I'm here to collect a cargo from the book warehouse. Johansson's…up stream. It is just through the dock. At the next wharf. There is the parchment.' I replied.

I pointed to a pile of parchments that had once been on the fold-down scribing desk and were now strewn across the floor.

'When did you arrive here?' He asked.

'Yesterday, about the third bell of the Dog Watch. Dusk.'

'Stay here.' He said as one of his men shouted to him from outside.

'Search for contraband.' He barked at the remaining constable.

The plod looked at me and smirked. The dibble climbed out of the cabin and on to the deck. He mounted the plank and moved swiftly to the bank. Ignoring his instructions I followed him. The plod accompanied me. He was obviously curious too.

The body was soggy, wet, and bloated. It lay like a white whale on the mud packed towpath. Small holes, the marks of rodents teeth, showed clearly on the its extremities and the torso showed a washer-woman's swelling and wrinkling. The dibble bent over the body and we crowded around morbidly curious to see the spectacle.

The man was small, about my height and he wore dark cotton leggings and a strange silk waistcoat. His long black hair was plaited into a pigtail. The pigtail had been cut-off just short of the base of his skull. I let out a gasp as the dibble turned him over.

The mans face had a pale waxy colouring ~ like a burnt out candle. The eyes had an epicanthic fold and were dark. Well one of them was. The other was missing. Only a length of the sinew remained. The holes in his cheeks, where the rodents had feasted, were a marbled and macerated pulp. A deep scar ran down from his ear to the jaw. The last three fingers from the right hand were also missing. A red dragon was tattooed on his lower right arm ~ the sleeve. It was climbing upwards along his lower arm, its tail looped around the wrist.

The dibble studied the body silently from top to bottom and back again. Finally returning to the head. He bent low over the face and pushed his fingers deep into the dead man's mouth. Slowly his fingers twisted and he extracted a piece of duckweed. It was as long as my forearm.

'He was alive when he went in.' Said the dibble looking up at me and nodding to the taller plod.

'Fancy finding weed in Camden Town.' I said.

Then the spears shaft cracked across the base of my skull.

4

Hitchin' A Ride

Robyn Nudd; and the Sheriff of Nottingham are journeying northwest from London on the Paddington Arm of the Grand Union Canal, North London, W1 9EH.

The water swirled darkly around the Sheriff as she settled within the lock. I grabbed the lock key and commenced making the preparations to open the upper gate. The Sheriff slowly floated upwards as the swirling water filled the lock. Soon the operation was complete. I placed my back on the gate's arm and heaving with all my might, my feet resting firmly on the raised stone ladder, I pushed. The lock gate began to swim in the water. Once it was open I pulled on the guide rope and the Sheriff drifted into the quayside. Quickly I un-tied the forward line. Then the aft line. I held the guideline taut as the Sheriff floated freely and then pulling hard, I brought the Sheriff forward. She slipped through the murky waters easily;

'Like a soul floating from one world to another.'

Coiling the guideline carefully, I stepped on to the aft deck, and gently slipped the gear lever to the forward position. The Sheriff's Perkins steam engine coughs slightly but she never fails me. She has a dual powered system. One that can be run from the wood burner or from the batteries, which in turn are charged by the solar panels along her roof. The batteries are also charged from the generator which is powered by the steam engine. Of course there is the Major too. He is a massive grey Yorkshire Shire horse. He is getting on in years now and is not always with me on my journeys but when he is…the year's fall away and he pulls her along the tow path with, what appears to be, effortless ease. The Sheriff also has a mast and short-rigged sail which I only use on the tidal part of the bigger rivers.

After resting for a moment, I gave a swift sweet toot on the whistle. The Sheriff moved gracefully out of the lock and we slipped upstream. It took ten more minutes to moor next to the lock, tie-up, and closed the upper gates. Then I studied the sky and made the decision to secure the mooring. We would stay put for the night.

I whistled and Ferdinand looked up from where he dozed on the roof. He leapt easily, landing on the bank. I stooped to collect a small hatchet and a large wicker basket, that also held a knife. Ferdinand and I strolled away from the lock and walked along the towpath. We moved slightly off to the left in the direction of a small coppice. The wood was a thin thing. I bent my head and I asked the gods of the trees to forgive me and let them know that the axe was only to divide the fallen and wind broken branches. It took only a short time and soon we had collected enough wood to keep the Sheriff's fire burning for a few days. Then we took the time to gather what we could forage from natures pantry; Wild Mushrooms, Garlic, Sorell, and Chives, and a few early Raspberries that grew thereabouts. The god's of the trees seemed to smile upon us and for once we came away without even a scratch from the brambles or a burr in our hair.

Once back aboard, I dropped lazily on to the bench and watched the skyline. The sun was dropping lower in the sky now. A murmuration of birds, probably starlings, formed high above in the evening sky and performed in an intricate swooping circle of dance. We watched in amazement.

'Now there's a strange sight Ferdi. The Lady Yvette told me that the birds dance when it is time for things to pass, like the death of winter and the coming of summer. Wonderful how they all speak to each other that way.'

Ferdinand raised an eyebrow and scowled at me. I had no idea what he was thinking. I tossed him a piece of cheese. He caught it mid-air and wolfed it greedily. I followed suit, eating a morsel myself. Then I found the wine bottles in the aft pokey hole. It was a good vintage. One that my friend, Jacqui Feather Ear, had brought over to the lock at Camden for me. I took a tumbler of the strong red wine and walked back to the aft bench and began chewing on an apple.

'She got this wine from some parson…out Wells-on-Sea way. This is wonderful init Ferdi? Not a soul in sight…and a beautiful evening to look forward to. I had forgotten it was May day…what with the quizzers and all.'

Ferdinand nodded and showed his agreement by caressing my leg gently. A gentle breeze stirred the peaceful night as it wafted down the canal and over the fields. The night progressed softly and soon darkness had fallen all about us. The moon began to rise, just north of true east, as the goddess Selene drove her chariot high into the night sky. It was a full, bright moon and as it passed behind a small cloud, a very strange thing happened. A wolf, somewhere in the night, began to sing and was joined by several others in an a cappella version of Fly Me To The Moon. Not something you tend to hear so close to a big city. I mentioned this to Ferdinand. He choked on his cheese.

The moon re-emerged from behind the cloud. The first slim crescent of it slowly becoming visible. Then a truly strange phenomenon took place. The upper horn of the moon's crescent seemed to split in to two and from the mid-point of the division, a bright flaming torch seemed to spring. It spewed out over a considerable distance ~ like a blast of fire with hot coals and sparks. The body of the moon, which was below, seemed to writhe. It reminded me of a wounded snake. This happened a dozen times or more. And as it emerged fully the moon it took on a dark hue. The whole round moon shone a deep, dark red. A Bloode Moon.

'Holy avenging angels!' I shrieked,
'The gods must be angered by something tonight!'
'It's the bloode moon Ferdi! Not something I thought I would ever see. Not in my lifetime. It's a sign that true evil is abroad!'

Jailhouse Blues

*Robyn Nudd; and the Sheriff of Nottingham are jour-
neying northwest from London on the Paddington Arm
of the Grand Union Canal, North London, N1. They are
accompanied by a mysterious dark fellow, who goes by
the name of Ferdinand de Noirfoncé.*

We sat under that dark red moon and sipped our
dark red wine. I shivered slightly although it was a
warm night. My thoughts drifted back to Clink Street
prison and the quizzers.

It had been four days since the ministry had released me from the cells. Once back aboard the Sheriff we had set sail immediately. We had called only
at Johanssons, the publishers, to collect the cargo
of books and parchment and then we made a quick
about turn and we were off ~ upstream towards
Oxford.

'You know they had me in that lockup for three
days and a half?' I said to Ferdinand; he was hitching
a ride with me and paying his fare by lending a hand.

'…'Course…soon as I got back I checked the pokey
holes. They had found some of the cheese and some
of the wine but that was all.' I laughed.

'They hadn't found the Sheriff's secret stashes.
They did make a right mess of her though. Plod 'n'
dibble.' I said patting the Sheriff's side lovingly.

'…but you know what got to me though, Ferdi? It

was the questions. The same questions. Over and over and over again. For nearly two days. The same damn questions!'

'What was I doing in Camden? How long had I been there? Where was I going? And who was the China-man?'

'Well I said to them; Chinaman? I don't know no Chinaman. How am I supposed to know the body was a Chinaman? I mean it could have been anyone. The state it was in! I told them…'

'…There was always the two of them working on me at any one time, with another team and they were changing it about every few hours. Then there was this sinister chap. Topcliffe he was called. Day two he turned up, I reckon…but I can't be sure. They did not let me sleep at all and the rooms were all dark and windowless.'

'Anyway, this sinister one, he was a youngish man, thinner, and smaller than most and really so very ordinary looking. Although to be honest I never got a proper good look at him.' I paused and took a drink of wine from the tumbler.

'Anyway, he just sat there in the shadows…listen-ing. Occasionally he would signal the quizzers and they would go over to him. He would whispered to them for a moment and when they came back it was…start again at the beginning…and then a dif-ferent question. Right out of the clear blue. Who was I meeting? What music did I like? How many China-men did I know?'

'Ministry. That's what he was. An true quizzer if ever I saw one. Then, after what seemed forever, this smallish chap comes in. He was different. Well dress in nice clothes like but not too fancy, ya know? He was quite attractive…in a quite sort of way. Not my normal type at all…but then I guess you know…I sail a different stream, ha. But to be fair there was something about him. He greets this Topcliffe sort with a handclasp and I kind of see's it's a secret signal. Like a secret grip…you know? Templar! That what I thought. Well you hear such stories…Jacqui Feather Ear told me…no, that's for later, anyway, like I was saying…he come up to me…right in front of me like and he just stands there and looks at me. Looks straight at me…for the longest time. Never blinking once…he didn't. Now, I know he wasn't no inquisitor nor the ministry type. I can smell them a mile off. Don't know who he was…but after looking at me for a good long while and without saying a single word he walks back to the Topcliffe guy in the corner, the ministry type, and he whispers something. Then the quizzers get new instructions…and they leave the room. This attractive quiet type of geezer comes over to me and sits there…silent like for a few more moments. Then he asks;'

'How often did I go to Cambridge?'

'Well nar and again, I says, when I has a contract with Johanssons the publishers. They sometimes 'as me to go. Quite often I suppose. Three times, maybe four times a year, maybe more…the universities, init? They have lots of books. It's been about six weeks since I last been. Slow…boat travel is, you know. But safest…North of the Gap.'

'So next he asks me if I like Chinese food? And what was my favourite nosh house? I tells him yes…I likes it all right. But not all of us can afford to eat in nosh houses.'

'Well, humour me, he says. And I'm staring right in to his deep blue eyes and I can see the little bits of yellow in them. So I says that I heard the Golden Sun was good…in China Town, back in Sheffield. And some of the street stalls in the shanty was all right too.'

'What about the Red Dragon in Soho? He asks me.'

'Never heard of it, I says. I don't do a lot of nightlife in London. Just stay local to Camden like. It's risky for a girl…on her own. I says.'

'Then…and get me here Ferdi. Then he asks; Where I got my tats done? My tats! And I know like it's not an approved trade. And the Ministry is down on 'em big time. So I says;'

'Just around…and at fairs and such. And he says to me. And listen to this Ferdi! He says;'

'I don't think so young lady. That is really quite good ink.'

'I mean…who is this guy? Some type of tattoo connoisseur?'

'So…I says…well yes. Now I remember…thinkin' about it proper like…back in the day…some of me mates had studied tattoo artistry…in Sheffield like. And they needed a model to work on.'

'Then…you listening Ferdi?'

Ferdinand just looked up, yawned, and slowly nodded his head.

'Well get me. Then he asks if he can look at 'em? So I show him me sleeves. He studies them real close. Turning my arms, gentle like, around and back…just to see the whole effect of the designs like.'

'Very nice, he said after a bit of study. Eventually he asked me;'

'Do you have any more tattoos young lady?'

'I looks at him…hard like…straight in the eyes and says, maybe…some.'

'How many?'

'Well…quite a lot really. So, Ferdi, listen to this! So he says,'

'Would I mind, being so kind, as to showing him the rest?'

'Well…now I could feel my nipples going hard! And me stomach…felt all kind of woozy…'cos like…if it had been him and me alone like… in a different place

like…it would have been…well. 'Cos, and I don't
mind telling you Ferdi, he had me motor running. If
you know what I mean.'
   'A kind of soft, gentle, twang he had. Hard to say
where he was from though. But he had defo spent
some time north of the gap. That's for sure. You
know? Certain words he used. But he was educated
too. So I knew he was…Empire or worse…Templar!'
   'So I smiled and says;'
   'Aren't you going to buy me dinner first?'
   'He just laughs. And his whole face was completely
different. Kind of…sort of a boyish grin he had. Not
like he was one of the ministry or even empire types
at all.'
   'And he says to me with a wink.'
   'Chinese?'
   'I had to laugh. He disappears then. Slipped back
into the shadows and speaks to the Topcliffe guy.'
   'The very next thing…they take me out and two
female plod has me stripped. Totally naked. And
then, this artist comes in and he starts making
drawings of me…and me tats. All of them! Each and
every single tattoo I ever had. Some…even I had
forgotten about. Well…I am telling you…there is not
that many souls alive that has seen all of me tats.
Not all at once anyway. Not recently…that's for sure.
It's been a long dry spell.' I smiled as I remembered
something completely different.
   'Next thing…I'm back. A different room. Up stairs
it was…with candles and wall torches and windows.
And with the quizzers from the afternoon shift. And
the nice guy. He is looking at the drawings of me.
Me…there in all me glory! And then he asks me about
the Art? That's the word he used…Art. Why this
symbol? Why these? And did I know anything about
the history of tattoos? Had I ever had one altered…
inked over or removed? he asked softly.'

'Quite painful, I've been told, he says...in that soft voice he had. Like liquid chocolate it was.'

'Anyway, I said no. And he looked at me. Straight on...if you know what I mean. And he picks up a drawing of me...a full frontal it was. And with a twinkle in his eyes he says;'

'Goodbye Miss Nudd. I hope this ordeal has not been to trying for you.'

'And he smiles at me. The he turns and leaves the room. And the Topcliffe man follows him out.'

'And I'm sure. For damn I'm sure that I saw him pocket that drawing. And if he did...that was a smooth bit of work. Defo not something you learn in one of those universities...and in front of the ministry man and a team of quizzers too. I'm telling you.' I said with admiration and took another drink of wine.

'Well he and the Topcliffe man...they just gets up and leaves. Followed by the team of monkeys. And a woman comes in and ask if I would like some food and a drink?'

'Next, it's all pals like...and if I could just tell them about the contraband...I could be on my way...and they were sure that, this time, it would just be a warning.'

'So I said; I know it was a bit dodgy like...but I took it in good faith...and I got it in barter...for giving some geezer a ride one day...on the Sheriff like...out Stratford way it was. Along the Grand Union. Came in handy he did. What with the Hatton Flight an' all. Twenty and three locks there...up that damned hill.'

'And they says; Well...as how to be more careful, as they say, this time it's just a warning, but if I am caught again, with contraband...it will be full on. Judge and jury time...and chokey...maybe worse. Maybe take a hand off too!'

I looked at my right hand and shuddered at the

thought.

'Still…I bet that cheese never left the Clink Street, eh Ferdi?'

'Never did see that nice geezer again. There was something so familiar about him. Like I already knew him…had met him somewhere maybe.' I smiled a fond smile.

'Who knows? On a different day…well you know.' I grinned, blushing a little. Which was unusual for me.

We sat and watched the bloode moon as Selene pulled it across the sky. It sent a shiver down my back. Ferdinand looked at me with one eye and shook his head sadly.

'One day. Dat girl gonna find a whole heap o' troubles…and ting.'

He stood, stretched, and strolled back into the cabin. He found a soft place on the couch. Then gave his tail a quick flick. He curled it around his feet and up towards his head and closed his eyes.

'Yes sir. A whole heap o' troubles.'

Disclaimer

This novel is a work of fiction which takes place in a fantasy world. A substantial amount of imagination and creativity has been employed to ensure that any similarity between names, characters, businesses, places, events, incidents, actual persons, alive or dead, in your world are completely and purely coincidental.

More Information

More information on the Alchemy Series, The Great Book of Alchemy, and other books featuring the Characters of the 5th Worlde Sagas can be found at the websites.

http://www.5thworlde.com
&
http://www.greatbookofalchemy.com

Also by the Author

The Alchemy Series

Book 1
The Work of Gods

Book 2
The Adventures of Robyn Nudd ~Part I
[Whole Heap O' Troubles]

Book3
The Worst Hero ~ Part II
[The Rise of Germania]

The Great Book of Alchemy

Part I
From The Devil We Came